White

Apple
Beluga Whale
Birch Trees
Daisies
Doves
Iceberg
Llama
Mechanitis Mimic
    Caterpillar
Moon
Mute Swan
Polar Bear
Sand Dollar
Zebra Swallowtail
    Butterfly

Gray

Chickadee
Chickadee Chicks
Box Turtle
Gray Squirrel
Great Gray Owl
Mouse
Pond
Rain
Red Tree
    Frog
Trees
Wolves
Woods

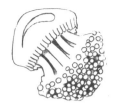

Pink

Clam Shell
Conch
Conch Pearls
Flamingo
Flower-mantis
Flowers
Jellyfish
Orchid
Pig
Pink Spotted
    Hawksmoth
Royal Gramma Fish
Spider
Tree Snail

Gold

Aspen
Autumn Leaves
Bear
California Poppies
Fawn
Honey
Honey Comb
Mandarin Duck
Wheat

Teal

American Robin Eggs
Blue Cheese
Caterpillar
Cone Headed Lizard
Mold
Parakeet
Parrotfish
Peacock
Poison Frog
Skipper Butterfly
Stink Bug

Brown

Armadillo
Abaco Barbs
Camel
Cattails
Chipmunk
Cow
Mallard Ducks
Peanuts
Spur Throated
    Grasshopper
Swamp Rabbit

Last Page

Madagascar Sunset
    Moth
Bi-color Poison Frog

COLOR,
COLOR,
Where Are You,
COLOR?

COLOR, COLOR, Where Are You, COLOR?

Mary Koski   Illustrated by Janeen Mason

To my pug dog, Gus, who helped me look at nature during our long walks.
- MK

For Robert and Irene Gernheuser, the best parents a child could hope to have.
Forever and ever,
- JM

Library of Congress Cataloging-in-Publication Data

Koski, Mary, 1951-
Color, color, where are you, color? / Mary Koski ; illustrated by Janeen I. Mason.–1st American ed.
  p.cm
Summary: Pictures of plants and animals illustrate colors from nature accompanied by rhyming text.
  Audience: Ages 4-8
   LCCN: 2004100445
   ISBN: 1-930650-35-3

1. Colors--Juvenile fiction. [1. Color--Fiction. 2. Stories in rhyme.] I. Mason, Janeen I. II. Title.

PZ8.3.K8514Col2004   [E]   QBI04-200039

Trellis Publishing, Inc.
P.O. Box 16141
Duluth, MN 55816
800-513-0115

First American Edition

10 9 8 7 6 5 4 3 2 1
Printed in China

Cover design by Janeen I. Mason
Interior layout by Gary Kruchowski
and John Burgraff

Color, color, where are you, color?
All around us in one form or another.
Mammals and plants,
the smallest of ants —
look all around you, and find lots of color.

Red, red, where are you, red?
Cherries and apples and hummingbird head.
Cardinals and fox,
tomatoes and phlox –
look all around you, and find something red.

Yellow, yellow, where are you, yellow?

Lemons and fishes and seahorsy fellow.

Lilies and corn,

daffodil horn –

look all around you, and find something yellow.

Blue, blue, can I find you?
   Bluebells and feathers and kitty eyes too.
   Oceans and lakes,
      blue jays and snakes –
   look all around you, and find something blue.

Orange, orange, can I find orange?
   Carrots and tigers and even a sponge.
      Monarchs and squash,
      puffins awash –
look all around you, and find something orange.

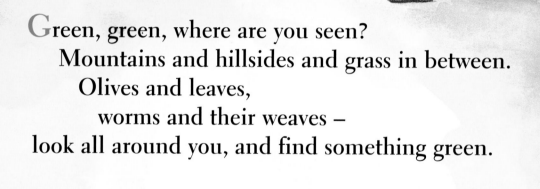

Green, green, where are you seen?
Mountains and hillsides and grass in between.
Olives and leaves,
worms and their weaves –
look all around you, and find something green.

Purple, purple, where are you, purple?
Crocus and eggplant and shark fins that ripple.
Parrots and grapes,
octopi shapes –
look all around you, and find something purple.

Black, black, where are you, black?
Seen on a skunk and a ladybug's back.
Penguins on snow,
crows in a row –
look all around you, and find something black.

White, white, are you this bright?
    Bears on an iceberg in moonlight at night.
        Llamas and birch,
        doves on a perch –
    look all around you, and find something white.

Gray, gray, are you at play?
     Wolves in the woods on a cloudy, wet day.
     Squirrels and sticks,
          chick-a-dee chicks –
look all around you, and find something gray.

Pink, pink, where are you, pink?
   Pink might be closer than you'd ever think.
   Orchids and pearls,
      pigs and their curls –
   look all around you, and find something pink.

Gold, gold, is your story told?
Poppies and aspen and honey to hold.
Wheat fields at dawn,
fur of a fawn –
look all around you, and find something gold.

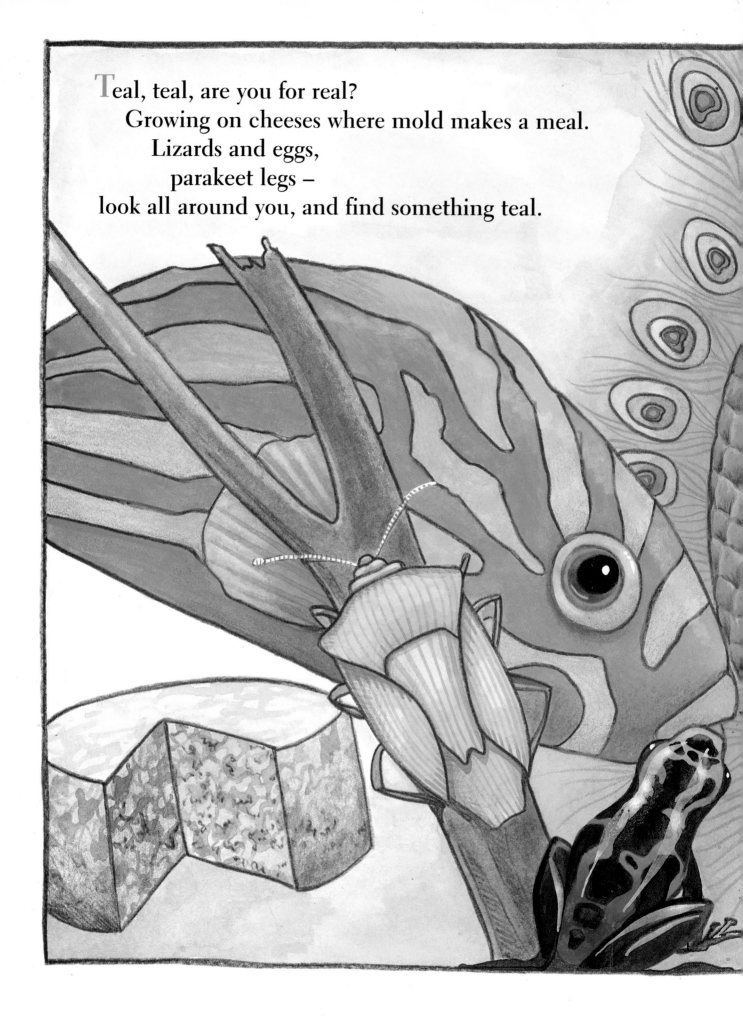

Teal, teal, are you for real?
    Growing on cheeses where mold makes a meal.
        Lizards and eggs,
        parakeet legs –
    look all around you, and find something teal.

Brown, brown, are you around?
   Horses and peanuts and ducks on the ground.
   Rabbits and cows,
     camel eyebrows –
   look all around you, and find something brown.

Color, color, where are you, color?
   All around us in one form or another.
      Country or town,
         look up and down –
   nature will help you to find lots of color.

First Page
Ants
Bluebird
Hibiscus

Red
Apple
Cardinal
Cherries
Coral Crab
Fox
Fuchsia
Lobster
Hummingbird
Maple Leaf
Onion
Phlox
Radishes
Soldierfish
Tomatoes
Watermelon

Yellow
Amberwing Dragonfly
Bananas
Corn
Daffodil
Giraffe
Honey Bee
Lemon
Lily
Seahorse
Tiger Swallowtail
    Butterfly
Trumpetfish

Blue
Blow Fly
Bluebells
Blueberries
Blue Jay
Blue Spruce
Common Morpho
    Butterfly
Dyeing Poison Frog
Indigo Snake
Kitten
Peacock Feather
Man-O-War
Man-O-War Fish
White's Tree Frog
Ocean
Lake

Orange
Carrots
Clownfish
Monarch Butterfly
Nautilus
Oranges
Puffin
Sea Star
Sponge
Squash
Tiger

Green
African Moon Moth
African Moon Moth
    Caterpillar
Alligator
Blue Claw Crab
Chrysalis
Grass
Green Bell Pepper
Jack in the Pulpit

Olives
Mountains
Pixie Cup Lichen
Scarab Beetle
Slant Faced
    Grasshopper
Superb Gaza Snail
Severe Macaw

Purple
Anemone
Sharks
Crocus
Eggplant
Gecko
Grapes
Hyacinth Macaw
Octopi
Octopi Ink
Prayer Plant
Purple Mort Bleu
    Butterfly

Black
Black Eyed Susan
Black Olives
Black Panther
Burchell's Zebra
Caterpillar
Crows
Fire Bellied Toad
King Penguin
Ladybug
Nerite Shells
Orca
Panda
Skunk
Tiger Salamander
Zebra Butterfly